Dear Parents and Teachers,

In an easy-reader format, **My Readers** introduce classic stories to children who are learning to read. Favorite characters and time-tested tales are the basis for **My Readers**, which are available in three levels:

1 **Level One** is for the emergent reader and features repetitive language and word clues in the illustrations.

2 **Level Two** is for more advanced readers who still need support saying and understanding some words. Stories are longer with word clues in the illustrations.

3 **Level Three** is for independent, fluent readers who enjoy working out occasional unfamiliar words. The stories are longer and divided into chapters.

Encourage children to select books based on interests, not reading levels. Read aloud with children, showing them how to use the illustrations for clues. With adult guidance and rereading, children will eventually read the desired book on their own.

Here are some ways you might want to use this book with children:

- Talk about the title and the cover illustrations. Encourage the child to use these to predict what the story is about.
- Discuss the interior illustrations and try to piece together a story based on the pictures. Does the child want to change or adjust his first prediction?
- After children reread a story, suggest they retell or act out a favorite part.

My Readers will not only help children become readers, they will serve as an introduction to some of the finest classic children's books available today.

—LAURA ROBB
Educator and Reading Consultant

For activities and reading tips, visit myreadersonline.com.

*Many thanks to Sonia Domingo Orevillo, for Miss Lina's
words of inspiration, and to Diana Rañola, for sharing
her expertise, and most of all, for friendship.*
—G.M.

SQUARE
FISH

An Imprint of Macmillan Children's Publishing Group

Square Fish books may be purchased for business or promotional use. For information on bulk purchases,
please contact the Macmillan Corporate and Premium Sales Department at (800) 221-7945 x5442
or by e-mail at specialmarkets@macmillan.com

Library of Congress Cataloging-in-Publication Data Available

ISBN 978-1-250-04716-8 (hardcover)
1 3 5 7 9 10 8 6 4 2

ISBN 978-1-250-04717-5 (paperback)
1 3 5 7 9 10 8 6 4 2

Book design by Patrick Collins/Véronique Lefèvre Sweet

Square Fish logo designed by Filomena Tuosto

Illustrations previously published in *Miss Lina's Ballerinas* by Feiwel and Friends,
an imprint of Macmillan.

First My Readers Edition: 2014

myreadersonline.com
mackids.com

This is a Level 1 book

Lexile 230L

A Day with Miss Lina's Ballerinas

By Grace Maccarone

Illustrated by Christine Davenier

SQUARE
FISH

Macmillan Children's Publishing Group

New York

The sun comes up.
The girls go in.

Miss Lina's class
can now begin.

The ballerinas jump.

They pose.

They bend and leap

and spin on toes.

One girl forgets
which step to do.
They all fall down—
Miss Lina, too.

"You must not be
afraid to fall," she says.

"The floor will catch you all."

Class is over.
On the street,
they go to school
on dancing feet.

The girls pass through the zoo.
They pose.

They pass the marketplace
in rows.

And at the park,
they dance on toes.

At school,
the ballerinas need
to dance at math . . .

and while they read.

At three o'clock,
the school day ends.

There's much more fun
for dancing friends.

At the park,
they make a pose . . .

at the market,

point their toes . . .

and at the zoo,

they dance in rows.

They dance back home
and dance to bed . . .

and dream
of dancing days
ahead.

Ballet Words

relevé

(reh-leh-VAY)

raised

jeté

(jeh-TAY)

thrown

pirouette

(pee-roo-ET)

spin

plié

(plee-AY)

bent

tendu

(tahn-DOO)

stretched